ILLUSTRATED ANIMAL CLASSICS

adapted by
GRAEME KENT

illustrated by
ERIC KINCAID

BRIMAX

INTRODUCTION

They seem to appear from everywhere, in all shapes and sizes, chattering, plotting, joking, fighting and making great decisions. They scurry out of bushes, pop up from holes in the ground, swing through the trees of forests, leap across ditches, and go in search of marvellous, far-off places.

They are the animals of fiction. But these beasts are different. They have been touched by magic. They possess great and unusual gifts. They can talk, change themselves into wonderful forms, become the trusted friends and allies of human beings, and play important parts in momentous events.

Some of the most fascinating animals in the pages of literature will be found in this book. The Cowardly Lion hurries along the yellow brick road with the Scarecrow and the Tin Woodman and discovers that he is braver than he thought. Pinocchio, a trusting little puppet who longs to be a boy, is swindled out of his money by a blind cat who can see, a lame fox who can run, and ends up in prison. A swallow, heading for the warm lands, lingers on to help a statue assist others, and as a result sacrifices its own life. Two dignified, important men find themselves transformed into storks; forget how to change themselves back again, and have to depend upon the efforts of an owl to solve their problems.

These are just a few of the glorious beasts we encounter in these stories. There is also a shy dragon who hates fighting, and refuses a challenge from St George; a water-baby who talks to fish and seals, and manages to rescue a lobster; a fox and a rabbit who keep playing tricks on one another.

These famous and well-loved stories are set as far apart as Arabia and the Deep South of America; Kansas and Never-Never Land. They have been written by such masters as Charles Kingsley, Kenneth Grahame, Oscar Wilde, Andrew Lang and Joel Chandler Harris, among others.

The stories in this collection have been selected and adapted by Graeme Kent, a primary school headmaster who has also been a producer of children's programmes for the BBC, and education consultant to six Third World nations. He is the author of over sixty books, published in a dozen different countries, and hundreds of television and radio scripts. His text-book series *Journey into Books* (Cassell) is used as an introduction to children's literature in many primary and middle schools.

CONTENTS

ISBN 0 86112 231 3
Published by BRIMAX BOOKS, CAMBRIDGE, ENGLAND.
Printed in Hong Kong

MR TOAD

by Kenneth Grahame

The animal friends of Mr Toad were very worried about him. Toad had gone mad over motor cars—buying them, driving them, and crashing them. For his own good he had to be made to stop. One fine morning, Rat, Mole and Mr Badger went to Toad Hall to talk to their friend.

They reached the drive of Toad Hall to find a shiny new motor-car of great size standing in front of the house. As they neared the door it was flung open, and Mr Toad, wearing goggles, cap, gaiters, and an enormous overcoat, came swaggering down the steps, drawing on his gloves.

"Hullo! come on, you fellows," he cried cheerfully. "You're just in time to come with me for a jolly—to come for a jolly—for a—er—jolly."

His hearty accent died away as he noticed the stern unbending looks on the faces of all his silent friends.

The Badger strode up the steps. "Take him inside," he said sternly.

"Now then," he said to the Toad, when the four of them stood together in the hall, "first of all, take those ridiculous things off!"

"Shan't!" replied Toad with great spirit.

"You two, take them off him," ordered Badger briefly.

They had to lay Toad out on the floor, kicking and calling all sorts of names, before they could get to work properly. Then the Rat sat on him, and the Mole took his motor-clothes off him bit by bit, and they stood him up on his legs again.

"You knew it must come to this, sooner or later, Toad," the Badger said sternly. "You've paid no attention to our warnings; you've wasted the money your father left you on cars; and you're giving us animals a bad name by your furious driving, your smashes and your rows with the police. Come with me, I'm going to give you a good talking-to."

He took Toad firmly by the arm and led him into another room, and closed the door behind them.

"*That's* no good," scoffed the Rat. "*Talking* to Toad will never cure him. He'll *say* anything."

Through the closed door they could hear the drone of Badger's voice. Presently it was joined by sobs from Toad, who was a very soft-hearted fellow.

After some three-quarters of an hour, the door opened and the Badger appeared, leading by the paw a very limp and sad-looking Toad.

"I'm pleased to say," announced the Badger, "that Toad has seen the error of his ways. He has promised to give up motor-cars. Tell them, Toad."

There was a long pause. Toad looked this way and that, while the other animals waited in grave silence. At last he spoke.

"No!" he shouted. "I'm *not* sorry. In fact I promise that the very first motor-car I see, poop-poop! off I go in it!"

"Very well, then," said the Badger firmly. "Take him upstairs you two, and lock him in. We're going to stay at Toad Hall until Toad promises to give up cars. Rat, telephone the garage and tell them to collect that monster outside."

For days the anxious animals kept a watch over Toad, taking it in turn to go out. One morning it was Rat's turn to be in charge. Badger and Mole had gone for a walk and Rat took Toad's breakfast up to him on a tray. He was greeted by a moan from the occupant of the bed.

"What's the matter, Toad?" asked the Rat.

"Oh, Rat," whispered a sad little voice. "Please step round to the village as quickly as possible—even now it may be too late—and fetch the doctor."

"A doctor! Oh, he must really be bad," the worried Rat said to himself, as he hurried from the room, not forgetting to lock the door behind him, and he set off for the doctor's house in the next village.

As soon as he heard the key turn in the lock, Toad hopped lightly out of bed. He watched the Rat disappear down the drive. Then, laughing heartily, he dressed as quickly as possible in the smartest suit he could lay his hands on, filled his pockets with cash from a drawer, then next, knotting the sheets from his bed together, tying one end of this rope round the leg of his bed, he scrambled out, slid lightly to the ground, and, taking the opposite direction to the Rat, marched off happily, whistling a merry tune.

At first he took bypaths, crossed many fields, and changed his direction several times. When he felt sure that he had thrown off any pursuers, he almost danced along the road in his satisfaction and conceit.

"Smart piece of work that!" he remarked to himself, chuckling. "Brain against brute force—and brain came out on top—as it's bound to do. Poor old Ratty! My! Won't he catch it when the others get back!"

Full of conceited thoughts such as these, Toad strode along, his head in the air, till he reached a little town, where the sign of "The Red Lion", swinging across the road half-way down the main street, reminded him that he was hungry. He marched into the inn, ordered the best lunch that could be provided and sat down to eat it in the coffee-room.

He was about half-way through his meal when an only too familiar sound coming down the street made him start trembling all over. The poop-poop! drew nearer and nearer, the car could be heard to turn into the inn-yard and come to a stop; Toad had to hold on to the leg of the table to conceal his emotion. Presently the party entered the room, hungry and talkative, boasting about their car. Toad listened eagerly, all ears, for a time; at last he could stand it no longer. Unseen, he slipped out of the room, paid his bill at the bar, and as soon as he was outside walked round quietly to the inn-yard. "There can't be any harm," he said to himself, "in my only just *looking* at it!"

No one else was around. The car stood in the middle of the yard. Toad walked slowly round it.

"I wonder," he said to himself presently, "I wonder if this sort of car *starts* easily?"

Next moment, hardly knowing how it came about, he found he had hold of the handle and was turning it.

As the familiar sound broke forth, the old passion seized Toad and completely mastered him, body and soul. As if in a dream he found himself, somehow, seated in the driver's seat; as if in a dream, he pulled the lever and swung the car round the yard and out through the archway; and, as if in a dream he increased his pace.

As he leapt forth upon the highroad he only knew that he was Toad once more, Toad at his best and highest, Toad the terror, the Lord of the lone trail, before whom all must give way or be smitten down.

"To my mind," observed the Chairman of the Bench of Magistrates cheerfully, "the *only* difficulty that presents itself in this case is, how can we make it really hot for the rogue and ruffian we see cowering in the dock before us. Let me see, he has been found guilty, on the clearest evidence, first, of stealing a valuable motor-car; secondly, of driving to the public danger; and thirdly of gross impertinence to the rural police. Mr Clerk, will you tell us, please, what is the stiffest penalty we can impose for each of these offences? Without, of course, giving the prisoner the benefit of any doubt, because there isn't any."

The Clerk scratched his nose with his pen. "Some people would consider," he observed, "that stealing the motor-car was the worst offence; and so it is. But cheeking the police undoubtedly carries the severest penalty; and so it ought. Supposing you were to say twelve months for the theft, which is mild; and three years for the furious driving, which is lenient; and fifteen years for the cheek, which was pretty bad sort of cheek, judging by what we've heard—those figures tot up to nineteen years."

"First rate!" said the Chairman.

"So you had better make it a round twenty years and be on the safe side," ended the Clerk.

"An excellent suggestion!" said the Chairman approvingly. "Prisoner! Pull yourself together and try to stand up straight. It's going to be twenty years for you this time. And mind, if you appear before us again, upon any charge whatever, we shall have to deal with you very seriously!"

Then the brutal minions of the law fell upon the hapless Toad and dragged him from the Court House, through the streets to the dungeon that lay at the end of the town. There at last they paused, where an old jailer sat fingering a bunch of mighty keys.

"Oddsbodikins!" said the Sergeant of Police, taking off his helmet and wiping his forehead. "Rouse thee, old loon, and take over from us this vile Toad."

The jailer nodded grimly, laying his withered hand on the shoulder of the miserable Toad. The rusty key turned in the lock, the great door clanged behind them. Toad was a helpless prisoner in the remotest dungeon, of the best-guarded keep, of the stoutest castle in all the length and breadth of Merry England.

When Toad found himself imprisoned in the dungeon, he flung himself full length on the floor and shed bitter tears, and gave himself to dark despair.

With laments like these he passed his days and nights for several weeks, refusing all meals. His plight struck the heart of the jailer's daughter, a pleasant and good-hearted girl. She took it upon herself to persuade Toad to eat, and even, in the end, to talk to her about himself and his past.

The jailer's daughter grew very sorry for Toad, and thought it a great shame that a poor little animal should be locked away for what seemed to her a very trivial offence. One morning she said,

"Toad, just listen, please. I have an aunt who is a washerwoman."

"There, there," said Toad graciously, "never mind; think no more about it. *I* have several aunts who *ought* to be washerwomen."

"Do be quiet a minute, Toad," said the girl. "My aunt does the washing for all the prisoners in this castle. She takes out the washing on Monday morning, and brings it in on Friday evening. This is a Thursday. Now this is what I think: you're very rich, at least you're always telling me so, and she's very poor. I think if she was properly approached, you could come to some arrangement by which she would let you have her dress and bonnet and so on, and you could escape from the castle as the official washerwoman. What do you say?"

"You are a good, kind, clever girl," said Toad. "Introduce me to your aunt, if you will, and I am sure we can come to some arrangement."

Next evening the girl ushered her aunt in to Toad's cell, bearing his washing pinned up in a towel. She had been prepared beforehand for what was to happen, and the sight of a few gold pieces left on the table by Toad were enough to persuade her.

In return for his cash, Toad received a cotton print gown, an apron, a shawl, and a black bonnet. At the old lady's request, Toad gently gagged and bound her, and left her in a corner of the cell.

"Now it's your turn, Toad," said the jailer's daughter. "Take off that coat and waistcoat of yours; you're fat enough as it is."

Shaking with laughter, she dressed him in her aunt's clothes, finishing by tying the strings of her own bonnet under his chin.

"You're the very image of auntie," she giggled. "Now, goodbye Toad, and good luck. Go straight down the way you came up."

With a quaking heart Toad left the cell on his bid for freedom.

He was soon agreeably surprised to find how easy it was. The washerwoman was plainly a popular figure. Each warder passed on the figure in the print dress and the black bonnet, with a kind word to the next guardian of the prison.

It seemed hours to Toad before he crossed the last courtyard, rejected the pressing invitations from the last guardroom, and dodged the outspread arms of the last warder, pleading for just one last embrace. But at last he heard the gate close behind him, and knew that he was free!

Dizzy with success Toad walked towards the lights of the town, not knowing in the least what he would do next, but certain of one thing, that he must remove himself as quickly as possible from this area.

As he walked along, his attention was caught by some red and green lights a little way off to one side of the town, and the sound of the puffing and snorting of engines. "Aha!" he thought, "this is a piece of luck! A railway station is the thing I want most in the world at the moment."

He made his way to the station accordingly, looked at a time-table and found that a train bound, more or less in the direction of his home, was due to start in half an hour. "More luck!" said Toad, his spirits rising rapidly, and went off to the booking-office to buy his ticket.

He gave the name of the station nearest Toad Hall, and searched for the necessary money. But here the cotton gown intervened and prevented his reaching his pockets. In a sort of nightmare he struggled with the dress, while other would-be passengers lining up behind him made unkind and impatient remarks.

At last—somehow—he burst through to where his waistcoat pocket should be situated, only to remember that his waistcoat and his jacket, containing all his money, had been left behind in his cell.

In his misery he made one last effort to carry the thing off, and with a return to his fine old manner, he said, "Look here! I find I've left my purse behind. Just give me that ticket, will you, and I'll send the money on tomorrow. I'm well-known in these parts."

The clerk stared at him and the dusty black bonnet for a moment, and then laughed. "I should think you are pretty well known in these parts," he said, "if you've tried this game often. Here, stand away from the window, please, madam; you're in the way of the other passengers!"

An old gentleman who had been prodding him in the back for some moments thrust him away and, what was worse, addressed him as his good woman, which angered Toad more than anything else.

Baffled and full of despair, he wandered blindly down the platform to where the train was standing, and tears trickled down each side of his nose.

As he walked he found himself opposite the engine, which was being oiled and wiped by its driver, a burly man with an oil-can in one hand, and a lump of cotton-waste in the other.

"Hullo, mother!" said the engine-driver, "what's the trouble?"

"O sir!" said Toad, crying afresh. "I am a poor, unhappy washerwoman, and I've lost all my money, and can't pay for a ticket, and I *must* get home tonight somehow, and whatever I am to do I don't know. O dear, O dear!"

"That's a bad business, indeed," said the engine-driver slowly. "Lost your money—and can't get home—and got some kids waiting for you, I dare say?"

"Any amount of 'em," sobbed Toad. "And they'll be hungry—and playing with matches— and upsetting lamps, the little innocents!—and quarrelling, and going on generally. O dear, O dear!"

"Well, I'll tell you what I'll do," said the good engine-driver. "You're a washerwoman to your trade, says you. Very well, that's that. And I'm an engine-driver, as you may well see, and there's no denying it's terribly dirty work. Uses up a power of shirts, it does, till my missus is fair tired of washing 'em. If you'll wash a few shirts for me when you get home, and send 'em along, I'll give you a ride on my engine. It's against the rules, but we're not so very particular in these out-of-the-way parts."

The Toad's misery turned into rapture as he eagerly scrambled up into the cab of the engine. The guard waved his welcome flag, the engine driver whistled in cheerful response, and the train moved out of the station. As the speed increased, and the Toad could see real fields on either side of him, and trees and hedges, and cows and horses, all flying past him, he thought how every minute was bringing him nearer to Toad Hall.

THE STORY OF CALIPH STORK

by Andrew Lang

The Caliph, the chief man in all old Baghdad, was resting one afternoon. The Grand Vizier, his chief helper, came to see him.

"Why do you look so anxious, my friend?" asked the Caliph.

"Alas," said the Grand Vizier, "outside the palace is a pedlar. He is selling many beautiful things, but I have so little money to spare."

For some time the Caliph had wished to give his friend a present, so he sent a slave to fetch the pedlar before him. When the pedlar arrived, he turned out to be a short stout man in very ragged clothes. He carried a box with all manner of wares inside: strings of pearls, rings, combs and richly mounted pistols.

The Caliph and his Vizier inspected everything. The Caliph chose some handsome pistols for himself and for the Vizier. Just as the pedlar was about to close his box, the Caliph saw a small drawer. He asked the pedlar if he had anything else to spare for sale.

The pedlar opened the drawer and took out a box containing some black powder and a scroll written in strange characters, which neither the Caliph nor the Vizier could read.

"I got these two items from another merchant," he said. "I don't know what they are, but they are of no use to me. You may buy them if you like."

The Caliph bought the powder and the scroll, and sent the pedlar away. Then he asked the Vizier if he knew of anyone who could read the writing on the scroll.

"There is an old man called Selim in the city," said the Vizier. "He knows every language under the sun. I shall send for him."

When Selim arrived he studied the scroll. "My lord," he said, "it is written in Latin."

"Well, let us hear what it means," said the Caliph.

The old man began to read aloud from the scroll. "Anyone who sniffs the powder in this box, and at the same time says the word 'Mutabor!', can turn himself into any creature he likes. He will understand the language of all animals. When he wishes to become a human being again, he must bow three times to the east and repeat the same word. He must be careful, when he takes the shape of some bird or beast, not to laugh, or he would forget the magic word and remain an animal for ever."

The Caliph was delighted. He gave Selim a splendid robe and made him promise not to tell anyone about the magic powder. Then he sent the old man away.

"Tomorrow," the Caliph told the Vizier, "we will go into the country, sniff the powder, and then hear what is being said in air, earth and water."

The next morning, the Caliph and the Vizier walked with the box through the town to a pond far out in the country. There they saw a stork walking up and down, hunting for frogs. At the same time they saw another stork high in the sky, flying towards the same spot.

"Why don't we turn ourselves into storks? Then we could talk to those two," said the Vizier.

"That's a good idea," said the Caliph, "but let us remember how we are to turn ourselves back into men again. We must bow three times to the east, and say 'Mutabor!'. If we do that we will return to our human form. But for Heaven's sake don't laugh, or we are lost!"

The second stork circled and then landed. Quickly the Caliph took out the box and sniffed at the powder. Then he handed the box to the Vizier, who did the same. Finally the two men cried together 'Mutabor!'.

At once their legs grew thin and red; their smart yellow slippers turned to clumsy stork's feet; long necks sprouted between their shoulders; their beards disappeared, and their bodies were covered with feathers.

Meantime the second stork had reached the ground. It first scraped its bill with its claw, stroked down its feathers, and then walked towards the first stork. The Caliph and the Vizier, now storks themselves, drew closer and listened to the other two talking.

"Good morning, Dame Longlegs. You are out early this morning."

"Yes indeed, dear Chatterbill. I am getting myself a little breakfast. May I offer you a joint of lizard?"

"A thousand thanks, but I am here for something else. I am to dance tonight at a party, and I have come here for a little practice." The young stork began to move about with the most wonderful steps. The Caliph and the Vizier looked on. When the dancing stork suddenly balanced on one leg and flapped her wings up and down, they each burst out laughing.

"That's the funniest thing I've ever seen," said the Caliph, wiping the tears from his eyes.

21

Suddenly the Vizier remembered that they had been warned not to laugh. He reminded the Caliph of this.

"O dear!" said the Caliph, suddenly serious. "It would be dreadful if we had to remain storks for the rest of our days. Do try and remember the word we have to say. I have forgotten it!"

"We must bow three times to the east and say 'M . . . mu . . . mu . . .'."

They turned to the east and started bowing till their bills touched the ground, but, oh horror—the magic word was quite forgotten. No matter how hard they tried, they could not remember it. The Caliph and the Vizier remained storks as they were.

They wandered sadly across the fields. In their misery they could not think what to do next. For several days they wandered about, living on fruit. They found that they did not care much for frogs and lizards. Their one comfort was the power of flight, so often they flew over the roofs of Baghdad to see what was going on there.

During the first few days they saw signs of many disturbances in the streets below. Men were fighting and shouting. But about the fourth day, as they sat on the roof of the palace, they saw a splendid procession passing in the streets below them. Drums and trumpets sounded, a man in a scarlet and gold mantle sat on a great horse, surrounded by slaves. He was followed by soldiers who shouted, "Hail, Mirza, the Lord of Baghdad!"

"Now that I have gone, my greatest enemy has become ruler of Baghdad," groaned the Caliph.

"Let us fly to the sacred city of Medina," said the Vizier. "Perhaps we shall find help there."

They rose from the palace roof, and spread their wings towards Medina. But flying was not yet an easy matter for them, and they soon grew tired.

"Oh!" gasped the Vizier, after a couple of hours. "I can go on no longer; you fly too quickly for me. Let us find somewhere to spend the night."

In a valley below them they saw an old ruin. It had once been a castle, but now only a few rooms remained. The two storks walked along the corridors, seeking a dry spot. Suddenly the Vizier stopped.

"I heard someone close sigh and moan," he whispered.

"I heard it too," said the Caliph. "The sound came from down there."

They both hurried down a dark passage and stopped outside a door. From within the room behind the door they heard sighs mixed with sobs. The two storks opened the door and went in.

On the floor of the ruined room, lit by the moonlight streaming in through one small barred window, sat a huge screech owl. Big tears rolled from its large round eyes. When it saw the storks it gave a joyful cry. It gently wiped the tears from its eyes with spotted wings, and to the great amazement of the two visitors addressed them in the human tongue.

"Welcome, storks!" she croaked. "You have come to save me."

"Oh, screech owl," said the Caliph sadly, "it looks as if you have suffered in the same way we have. There is little that we can do to help anyone. Listen to our story."

In a few short sentences the Caliph told the owl how he and the Vizier had become storks. When he had finished the screech owl shook her head.

"My story is as sad as yours," she sighed. "I am the daughter of the King of the Indies. One day a wicked magician gave me a drink which changed me into an owl. That magician brought me to this horrible place, and told me that here I must stay until someone of his own free will asks me to marry him. Since then many months have passed and I have been forced to live here as an owl."

The Caliph fell into deep thought on hearing this story of the princess. "If I am not much mistaken," said he, "there is some connection between our misfortunes, but I do not know what."

"I think I know of a way in which we might save ourselves," said the owl excitedly. "Once a month the wicked magician who turned me into a bird comes to these ruins. Near here is a large hall in which he feasts with his companions. They tell each other all about their evil deeds. It is possible that they will mention the magic word which will turn you back into humans."

"Oh, dearest Princess," begged the Caliph, "tell me when he comes and where this hall is."

"Do not think me unkind," said the owl, "but I will do that on one condition. I want to be free too. One of you must offer to marry me."

The storks were rather taken aback by this. The Caliph and the Vizier went out of the room to talk together.

"Grand Vizier," said the Caliph, "this is a tiresome business. However, you can marry her."

"Oh yes, indeed?" answered the Vizier, "what do you think my wife would do if I took a princess home? She would scratch my eyes out. Besides, you are both young and unmarried."

They argued on for some time, but in the end when the Caliph saw that the Vizier would rather remain a stork to the end of his days than marry the owl, he agreed to propose to the bird himself. The owl was delighted. She told the two storks that the magician was due to arrive that very night.

She then led the Caliph and the Vizier to the hall. They passed through a long dark passage until a bright ray of light shone before them. The owl told her companions to keep very quiet.

Through a gap near where they stood, they could see the whole of the hall. It contained many fine pillars. In the middle of the hall stood a round table covered with dishes of food. Around the table sat eight men. One of them was the pedlar who had sold the Caliph the powder.

The man next to the pedlar begged him to tell of his latest doings. The pedlar then told the story of the Caliph and the Vizier.

"And what kind of word did you give them?" asked another of the wicked magicians at the table.

"An old Latin word; it is 'Mutabor'," said the pedlar.

As soon as the storks heard this they were overjoyed. They ran at a great pace to the door of the ruined castle. When they reached it the Caliph turned to the owl. "We are very grateful to you. Please take me as your husband."

Then he turned towards the east. Three times the storks bowed their heads to the sun, which was just rising over the mountains.

"Mutabor!" they both cried, and in an instant they were changed back into their old forms. The Caliph and the Grand Vizier fell weeping and laughing into each other's arms. Who shall describe their surprise when they turned round and saw standing before them a beautiful lady in a fine gown.

With a smile she held out her hand to the Caliph, and asked "Do you not recognise your screech owl?"

It was she! The Caliph was so enchanted by her grace and beauty, that he cried out that being turned into a stork had been the best piece of luck that had ever befallen him.

The three set out at once for Baghdad. The Caliph had enough gold in his purse to buy in the nearest village all that they needed for their journey. So at last they reached the gates of Baghdad.

Here the Caliph's arrival created a great sensation. His people had given him up for dead, and now they rejoiced to see their beloved ruler again.

The Caliph ruled long and happily with his wife the Princess. His merriest time was when the Grand Vizier visited him in the afternoon. When the Caliph was in high spirits he would imitate the Vizier's appearance when he was a stork. He would strut gravely with stiff legs up and down the room, chattering and showing how he had vainly bowed to the east and cried "Mu . . . Mu . . ."

The Caliph's wife and their children were always much entertained by this show, but if the Caliph carried on too long, the Vizier would take him to one side, and with a laugh threaten to tell the Caliph's wife how the Caliph had once tried to persuade the Grand Vizier to marry the screech owl instead!

BRER RABBIT AND BRER FOX

by Joel Chandler Harris

Brer Rabbit and Brer Fox lived with many other animals on a patch of countryside, where the sun was usually shining. These two animals did not like one another very much. They were always trying to play tricks on each other. Brer Fox was stronger than Brer Rabbit, but Brer Rabbit could think faster.

One day, a group of animals were clearing a patch of land to plant some crops. Brer Rabbit got very hot. He did not like to tell the others, in case they thought he was lazy, so he shouted out that he had got a thorn in his paw and would have to stop work for a while.

Quietly he slipped away, looking for somewhere cool to rest. After a while he came across a deep well, with a bucket hanging in it.

"That looks cool," said Brer Rabbit. "I'll just take a rest in that bucket."

With that he jumped into the bucket. At once the rope tied to the bucket began to unwind and the bucket went down into the well. Brer Rabbit was frightened. He knew where he came from, but he didn't know where he was going. Suddenly he felt the bucket hit the water. He sat very still, shaking and shivering in spite of himself.

Brer Fox had seen Brer Rabbit slip away and had followed him to see what he was up to now. He had watched while Brer Rabbit had jumped into the bucket and the bucket had descended into the well.

"Well, if that don't beat everything," said Brer Fox. "I reckon Brer Rabbit must keep his money hidden down in that well. Or maybe he's found a gold-mine. Anyway, I'm going to see for myself."

Brer Fox crept up closer to the well. Then he peered down into it. He couldn't see or hear anything. At the bottom of the well, Brer Rabbit was still too scared to move.

"Hey, Brer Rabbit!" called out Brer Fox. "I know you're down there. What are you doing?"

"Who? Me? Oh, I'm just fishing," called Brer Rabbit. "I was going to surprise you all by bringing a pile of fish back with me for our supper."

"Are there many down there, Brer Rabbit?"

"Lots of 'em, Brer Fox. The water's alive with fish. Come down and help me haul them in."

"How am I going to get down?" shouted Brer Fox.

"There's another bucket up there. It'll fetch you down all safe and sound."

Brer Rabbit sounded so happy that Brer Fox jumped into the other bucket. This bucket was tied to the other end of the rope which passed over a tree trunk above the top of the well. This meant that as the heavy Brer Fox went down, his weight pulled Brer Rabbit up.

When they passed each other at the half-way mark, Brer Rabbit sang out:

"Goodbye, Brer Fox, take care o' your clothes,
For this is the way the world goes;
Some goes up and some goes down,
You'll get to the bottom all safe and soun'."

As soon as Brer Rabbit got to the top of the well, he jumped out of the bucket and ran off to the farmer who owned the well, and told him that Brer Fox was down at the bottom, getting the water dirty. Then he hurried back to the well, and shouted down to Brer Fox:

"Here comes a man with a great big gun—
When he haul you up, you jump and run."

Brer Fox did just this, managing to run off into the trees before the farmer could shoot him when he pulled the bucket up. Before long, both animals were working back on the patch of ground again, just as if they had never heard of the well. But every now and then Brer Rabbit would burst out laughing, and Brer Fox would scowl and say nothing at all.

A day or two later, Brer Fox and Brer Bear were walking back from their gardens carrying some cabbages in two baskets. Who should they see but Brer Rabbit, asleep under a tree.

"I've got you this time!" shouted Brer Fox, and he jumped on Brer Rabbit and stuffed him into the pocket of his coat.

"What's happening?" squealed Brer Rabbit, waking up.

"I've caught you at last, that's what's happened," cried Brer Fox. "That'll teach you to go to sleep where I can find you."

"Let me out!" pleaded Brer Rabbit.

"You stay where you are, I've got plans for you," said Brer Fox, and he and Brer Bear went walking off together, carrying their baskets of cabbages.

It was not long before the two animals reached Brer Bear's house. The bear invited the fox in for a drink of honey-syrup. They went inside and put down their baskets.

Suddenly Brer Rabbit jumped out of Brer Fox's pocket, and went running round the room.

"You can run all you want to," sneered Brer Fox. "The doors and windows are shut. I'll find you wherever you go."

Without a word Brer Rabbit ran under the bed. There was a mat there. He scurried underneath it and lay still, his heart pumping.

"Is that the best you can do?" laughed Brer Fox, peering under the bed. "I can see your hump in that mat. You stay there till I'm ready for you."

Brer Rabbit still said nothing. He stayed under the mat until he heard Brer Bear pouring Brer Fox his drink. Then he wriggled out from under the mat and looked all about him.

On the other side of the bed were Brer Bear's slippers. Brer Rabbit took these in his mouth and slipped them under the mat. Then he sat back and looked at the hump they made. It looked as if he was still hiding under the mat himself!

Brer Rabbit smiled contentedly. It looked as if he was going to fool that old fox yet again. Quietly he crept towards the basket of cabbages that Brer Fox had left in a corner. While Brer Fox was talking to Brer Bear the rabbit crept into the basket and hid himself under the cabbages.

"Keep an eye on that rabbit under the carpet," he heard the fox say to the bear. "I'll just take my cabbages back home and put them in the stewpot. Then I'll come back and we can prepare ourselves a nice rabbit pie!"

With that Brer Fox picked up his basket of cabbages and carried his burden out of the house, and through the wood on the way to his home. He had not gone very far when Brer Rabbit gave a great groan in the bottom of the basket.

"Oooooh!" he moaned. "Ooooooh!"

"My goodness!" said Brer Fox, stopping and looking round in alarm. "What was that?"

"Oooooooh!" groaned Brer Rabbit again, now enjoying himself.

"It sounds as if it's coming from my basket," quavered a terrified Brer Fox. "I'm carrying some talking cabbages!"

"Ooooooh!" said Brer Rabbit as loudly as he could. "Put me down!"

"It is the cabbages!" shouted Brer Fox, dropping the basket with a thump.

Quickly Brer Rabbit punched two holes in one of the cabbage leaves and pushed his two eyes through them, glaring at the shaking Brer Fox. The fox screamed and jumped in the air.

"Those cabbages don't only talk, they've got eyes!" he screamed, and turned and ran off as fast as he could.

Brer Rabbit waited until the fox had reached the end of the track, then he came out from behind the cabbage leaf and called after the other animal. Brer Fox stopped and turned round. His jaw dropped open when he saw Brer Rabbit waving casually at him.

"Thanks for the ride, old friend," called out the rabbit, and picking up one of the cabbages for his lunch he disappeared among the trees, leaving Brer Fox behind him.

Brer Fox decided that it was time he got his own back on Brer Rabbit, so he set out to make a fool of him. He got some tar and turpentine and mixed it together. From this mixture he made a Tar Baby, a life-sized, black doll that was very sticky.

Brer Fox took the Tar Baby out into the road and placed it there. Then he went and hid in the bushes, where he could see what would happen.

It was not long before Brer Rabbit came hopping down the road. Brer Fox lay low. Brer Rabbit pranced along until he saw the Tar Baby. Then he reared up on his hind legs in astonishment. Brer Fox still lay low.

"Good morning," said Brer Rabbit to the Tar Baby. "Nice weather we're having."

The Tar Baby said nothing, and Brer Fox lay low.

"How are you feeling today?" went on the rabbit.

Still the Tar Baby said nothing. Brer Rabbit began to get cross.

"Are you deaf?" he asked sharply. "'Cause if you are, I can shout, you know."

The Tar Baby did not move, and Brer Fox lay low.

"You're stuck up, that's what you are," decided Brer Rabbit. "Think you're too good for me, huh? I'm going to cure that!"

Brer Fox chuckled to himself, but the Tar Baby said nothing, and did not move.

"I'm going to teach you how to meet respectable folk," said Brer Rabbit. "I'm going to do that if it's the last thing I do. If you don't take off your hat and say 'Howdy!', I'm going to bust you wide open."

The Tar Baby did not move, and Brer Fox lay low in the bushes, trying not to laugh.

Brer Rabbit kept on asking the Tar Baby to speak to him, and the Tar Baby said nothing. In the end Brer Rabbit got so wild that he drew back his fist and hit the Tar Baby on the side of the head. His fist stuck fast there and he could not pull it free.

"If you don't let go of me, I'll hit you again!" shouted Brer Rabbit. With that he hit the Tar Baby on the other side of the head with his other fist. That stuck there as well, and Brer Rabbit could not pull his fists away from the tar.

"Turn me loose, or I'll kick the stuffing out of you!" shouted Brer Rabbit, but the Tar Baby stood still and said nothing.

Brer Rabbit kicked out with both feet. They stuck to the Tar Baby as well. Then Brer Rabbit said that if the Tar Baby did not let him go he would butt him with his head. The Tar Baby stood still, so Brer Rabbit hit him with his head. That got stuck too!

Just then Brer Fox sauntered casually out of the bushes.

"Hi there, Brer Rabbit," he said. "You look kind of stuck-up this morning!"

Then Brer Fox rolled on the ground and laughed and laughed until he could laugh no more.

THE TIGER

by William Blake

Tiger! Tiger! burning bright
In the forests of the night,
What immortal hand or eye
Could frame thy fearful symmetry?

In what distant deeps or skies
Burnt the fire of thine eyes?
On what wings dare he aspire?
What the hand dare seize the fire?

And what shoulder, and what art,
Could twist the sinews of thy heart?
And when thy heart began to beat,
What dread hand? and what dread feet?

What the hammer? what the chain?
In what furnace was thy brain?
What the anvil? what dread grasp
Dare its deadly terrors grasp?

Then the stars threw down their spears
And watered heaven with their tears,
Did he smile his work to see?
Did he who made the Lamb make thee?

Tiger? Tiger? burning bright
In the forests of the night,
What immortal hand or eye
Dare frame thy fearful symmetry?

THE RELUCTANT DRAGON

by Kenneth Grahame

Hundreds of years ago there was a dragon who hated fighting. He let all the fighting dragons get on with it and went to live in a cave near a village. He spent all his time there writing poems and playing with his young friend, the Boy.

One day a stranger rode into the village. When the Boy found out who he was, he ran up the hill to the cave.

"It's all up, Dragon!" he shouted, as soon as he was within sight of the beast. "He's coming! He's here now! You'll have to pull yourself together and do something at last!"

The dragon was licking his scales and rubbing them with a bit of cloth the Boy's mother had lent him, till he shone like a great green jewel.

"Who's coming, Boy?" he yawned, without looking round.

"It's only St George who's coming, that's all," panted the Boy. "He's got the longest, wickedest-looking spear you ever did see. And it's his job to fight dragons, and kill 'em." And the Boy began to jump around in sheer delight at the prospect of this battle.

"O deary, deary me," moaned the dragon, "this is too awful. I won't see him, and that's flat. I don't want to know the fellow at all. You must tell him to go away at once, please."

"Now Dragon, Dragon," begged the Boy. "You've *got* to fight him some time or other, you know, 'cos he's St George and you're the dragon. Better get it over with."

36

"My dear little man," said the dragon, "just understand once and for all that I can't fight and I won't fight. I've never fought in my life, and I'm not going to start now."

"But if you don't fight he'll cut your head off," gasped the Boy, miserable at the prospect of losing both his fight and his friend.

"Oh, I think not," said the dragon in his lazy way. "You'll be able to arrange something. I've every confidence in you, you're such a *manager*. Just run down to the village, there's a good chap, and make it all right. I leave it entirely to you."

The Boy made his way back to the village. He entered the inn and went through to the room where St George sat.

"May I come in, St George?" said the Boy politely, as he paused at the door. "I want to talk to you about the dragon."

"Yes, come in, Boy," said the Saint kindly. "Another tale of misery and wrong, is it? Whom do you want avenged?"

"Nobody," said the Boy quickly. "The fact is, this is a *good* dragon."

"What do you mean?" frowned the Saint.

"Well, he's a friend of mine, and tells me the most beautiful stories you ever heard, all about the old times and when he was little. And he's kind. He's as engaging and as trustful and as simple as a child."

"I see," mused St George. "Perhaps I've misjudged the animal. But what are we to do?"

"I suppose you couldn't go away quietly, could you?" asked the Boy hopefully.

"Impossible, I fear," said the Saint. "Quite against the rules."

"Well then, look here," said the Boy. "Would you mind strolling up with me and seeing the dragon and talking it over. It's not far, and any friend of mine will be welcome."

"Well, it's irregular," frowned the Saint, "but it does seem sensible. All right, I'll come and talk to your dragon."

"I've brought a friend to see you, Dragon," said the Boy loudly.

The dragon woke up with a start. "I was just-er-thinking about things," he said in his simple way. "Very pleased to meet you, sir."

"This is St George," said the Boy shortly. "St George—the dragon."

"Don't you think," said St George in his pleasant way, "that the best plan would be just to fight it out? After all, I could make you."

"No, you couldn't," said the dragon firmly. "I should only go into my cave and hide down the hole in there. You'd soon get sick of hanging about waiting for me to come and fight."

St George gazed for a while at the fair plain around them. "This would be a great place for a fight," he sighed.

"But you see, I don't like fighting," explained the dragon.

"Then why don't we pretend to fight?" suggested the Saint. "I could spear you somewhere it wouldn't hurt, and that would be that."

"Could you do that?" asked the dragon, suddenly interested.

"Oh yes, there's such a lot of you that there must be a few spare places somewhere. Under the neck, for example—all those thick folds of skin. I could spear you there, and that would be that."

"Then what would happen?" asked the dragon.

"Well, according to the rules I should lead you in triumph to the village."

"And then?"

"Oh, there'll be shouting and speeches and things."

"Quite so," said the dragon. "And then?"

"Oh, and then," said St George, "why, and then there will be the usual feast, I suppose."

"Good," said the dragon, "and that's where *I* come in. Look here, I'm bored to death up here. I shall meet a lot of people at this feast. They'll see what a fine chap I am. I shall make a lot of friends. Very well, St George, the fight is on!"

St George and the Boy walked back down the hill. Suddenly the Saint stopped.

"*Knew* I'd forgotten something," he said. "There ought to be a Princess. Terror-stricken and chained to a rock, and all that sort of thing. Boy, can't you arrange a Princess?"

The Boy was in the middle of a great yawn. "I'm tired to death," he wailed, "and I *can't* arrange a Princess, or anything more, at this time of night. Anyway, my mother's sitting up for me, and *do* stop asking me to arrange things till tomorrow!"

Next morning, at quite an early hour, large numbers of people began streaming up to the Downs. They were dressed in their Sunday clothes and carried baskets of food and drink.

The Boy had a good front place, well up towards the cave. He was feeling anxious. Could the dragon be depended upon? He might change his mind and stay inside.

St George's red plumes topped the hill, as the Saint rode slowly forth to a great level place in front of the cave. Very gallant and beautiful he looked on his tall war-horse, his golden armour glancing in the sun, his great spear held erect, the little white pennon, crimson-crossed, fluttering at its point. He drew rein and waited.

"Now then, Dragon," muttered the Boy.

A low muttering, mingled with snorts, now made itself heard, rising to a bellowing roar that seemed to fill the plain. Then a cloud of smoke hid the mouth of the cave. Out of the midst of it the dragon himself, shining, magnificent, pranced forth.

Everybody said "oo-oo-oo!" as if he had been a mighty rocket. His scales were glittering, his long spiky tail lashed his sides, his claws tore up the turf and sent it flying over his back, and smoke and fire jetted from his nostrils.

"Oh, well done, Dragon!" cried the Boy. "Didn't think he had it in him," he added to himself.

St George lowered his spear, bent his head, dug his heels into his horse's side, and came thundering over the turf. The dragon charged with a roar and a squeal.

"Missed!" yelled the crowd. There was a moments tangle of golden armour and blue-green coils and spiky tail, and then the great horse, tearing at his bit, carried the Saint, his spear swung high in the air, almost up to the mouth of the cave.

The dragon sat down and barked viciously. St George pulled his horse round into position.

"End of Round One!" thought the Boy. "How well they managed it! But I hope the Saint won't get excited. I can trust the dragon all right. What a play-actor the fellow is."

St George managed to get his horse to stand steady, and was looking round him as he wiped his brow. Catching sight of the Boy, he smiled and nodded and held up three fingers for an instant.

"It all seems to be planned out," said the Boy to himself. "Round Three is to be the last one. Wish it could have lasted a bit longer. What's that old fool of a dragon doing now?"

The dragon was showing off, running round and round in circles, sending waves and ripples of movement along his spine, from his pointed ears right down to the spike at the end of his long tail.

St George gathered up his reins and began to move forward, dropping the point of his spear and settling himself in his saddle.

"Time!" yelled everybody excitedly.

The dragon sat up on end and began to leap from one side to the other. This made the horse swerve. The Saint only just saved himself by the mane; and as they shot past, the dragon delivered a vicious snap at the horse's tail which sent the poor beast running madly far over the Downs.

The crowd began to cheer the dragon, who strutted to and fro, his chest thrust out and his tail in the air, enjoying his new popularity.

St George had dismounted and was telling his horse exactly what he thought of him. The Boy made his way down to the Saint and held his spear for him.

"It's been a jolly fight, St George!" he said, with a sigh. "Can't you let it last a bit longer?"

"Well, I think I'd better not," said the Saint. "The fact is, your simple old friend's getting conceited now they're cheering him. He'll forget about our arrangement and start playing the fool. Then there's no telling where he would stop. I'll just finish him off in this round."

He swung himself into his saddle and took his spear from the Boy.
"Now don't you worry," he said kindly. "I've marked the spot exactly,
and the dragon's bound to help, because he wants to go to the feast."

St George trotted smartly towards the dragon and circled round
him. The dragon did the same, circling round the Saint. So the two
waited for an opening, while the spectators watched in breathless
silence.

There was a sudden movement of the Saint's arm, and then a
whirl of confusion of spines, claws, tail, and flying bits of turf. The
dust cleared away, the spectators whooped and ran in cheering. The
Boy saw that the dragon was down, pinned to the earth by the spear,
while St George had got off his horse and was standing over him.

It all seemed so real that the Boy ran up, hoping the dear old dragon wasn't hurt. As he approached, the dragon lifted one large eyelid, winked, and collapsed again. He was held fast to the earth by the neck, but the Saint had hit him in the spare place agreed upon, and it didn't even seem to tickle.

"Ain't you going to cut 'is 'ed orf, master?" asked one of the crowd. He had bet on the dragon to win, and was feeling a little sore.

"Well, not *today*, I think," said St George pleasantly. "You see, that can be done at *any* time. There's no hurry at all. I'll give him a good talking-to, but first I think we should all go down to the village and have some refreshment."

At that magic word *refreshment* the whole crowd lined up and waited for the signal to start. St George hauled on his spear with both hands and released the dragon. The dragon rose and shook himself and ran his eye over his spikes and scales and things to see that they were all in order. Then the Saint mounted and led everyone down the hill to the village. The dragon followed meekly behind with the Boy.

There were great doings when they got to the village again. St George made a speech in front of the inn. He told the crowd that he had tamed the dragon for them, and the dragon was willing to settle down and be a friend to everyone, so *they* must all make friends with *him* as well.

Then the Saint sat down amid great cheers. The dragon nudged the Boy in the ribs and told him that he couldn't have done it better himself. Then everyone went off to get ready for the feast.

It turned out to be a most pleasant affair. St George was happy because there had been a fight and he hadn't had to kill anybody. The dragon was happy because there had been a fight, and so far from being hurt in it, he had become very popular. The Boy was happy because there had been a fight and in spite of it, both his two friends were on the best of terms. And all the others were happy because there had been a fight, and—well—they didn't need any other reason for their happiness.

At last the feast was over, the guests had left, and only St George, the Boy and the dragon were left. The dragon had fallen asleep over the table.

"Come on, Dragon," said St George firmly. "The Boy is waiting to take you home, and so am I."

They woke the dragon and set off up the hill arm-in-arm, the Saint, the dragon and the Boy. The lights in the little village began to go out; but there were stars and a late moon, as they climbed to the Downs together. As they turned the last corner and disappeared from view, snatches of an old song were carried back on the night breeze. I can't be certain which of them was singing, but I *think* it was the dragon.

THE BLIND CAT AND THE LAME FOX

by Carlo Collodi

Pinocchio was a puppet made of wood. He had a long nose and he could run and jump as well as any boy. He dearly wanted to be a boy, and he was as naughty as any child. He ran away from the man who had carved him, and had many adventures. At the end of them he had managed to save five gold pieces. He decided that he had had enough of wandering and that he would go back home.

He had not gone far when he met two strange creatures on the road. There was a fox who was lame in one foot, and a cat who was blind. They helped each other along. The fox leaned on the cat and told her which way to go.

"Where are you going?" asked the fox pleasantly.

"I'm going home," Pinocchio told the two animals proudly. "I'm rich; I've got five gold pieces."

He showed them the money. The fox's lame paw reached out, and the cat's eyes opened wide for a moment, but Pinocchio did not notice.

"Pray, what will you do with all that money?" asked the fox.

"I shall buy a beautiful new coat for the man who made me," said Pinocchio, "and then I shall buy myself a book, so that I can go to school and learn things."

"You don't want to do that," said the cat at once. "Learning things can be very bad for you."

A bird which was singing in a hedge suddenly stopped warbling and said, "Pinocchio, don't listen to these two bad animals!"

In one swift movement the cat had jumped on the bird and had eaten it. Then quickly she closed her eyes and pretended to be blind again.

"What did you do that for?" asked Pinocchio.

"To teach him a lesson," said the cat. "Birds should not interrupt when their betters are talking."

"Talking of money," said the fox, "would you like to make yours much bigger?"

"How could I do that?" asked Pinocchio.

"We know a special place," said the cat.

"It's called the Field of Miracles," said the fox. "Anyone who has a gold piece may bury it there and leave it. During the night a tree of gold pieces will sprout up from where the one gold piece is buried."

"Really?" asked the astounded Pinocchio. "Suppose I buried my five gold pieces? How many would I get in return?"

"Thousands," said the cat. "Simply thousands."

"That's marvellous!" shouted Pinocchio. "Please take me there. If you do, I'll give you a present of some of the gold pieces that grow on the trees there."

"Certainly not!" said the cat offended.

"We wouldn't dream of taking a present from you," said the fox.

"We shall take you to the Field of Miracles because we like you," said the cat. "Come this way."

The three of them walked a long way for the rest of the day. Just as night was falling they came across an inn and decided to spend the night there. They entered the inn and had a good meal, and then went to their rooms to sleep.

Pinocchio did not have a good night. He kept dreaming about trees growing in fields, and each tree bearing many gold pieces, instead of leaves.

He woke up very early, while it was still dark, and went down the stairs to the inn.

"Are my friends up yet?" he asked the landlord.

"Up and left," said the man. "They didn't want to disturb you, so they said they would wait for you at the Field of Miracles. It's straight across the fields opposite the inn."

"Did they pay the bill?" yawned Pinocchio.

"Oh no! To do so would have been an insult to you. That's one gold piece, please."

Pinocchio gave up one of his pieces of gold and went outside. It was very dark and he had to feel his way across the fields. Only a few birds swooped in front of him and then were gone again.

For an hour or so Pinocchio made his way slowly in the direction of the Field of Miracles. He was passing a small clump of trees when two figures leapt out on him. They were both wrapped in charcoal sacks. It seemed to Pinocchio that the figures were oddly familiar, but he could not remember where he had seen them before. Quickly he placed his four remaining pieces of gold under his tongue.

"Your money or your life!" demanded the taller of the two figures, seizing Pinocchio.

The puppet made signs with his hands, as if to say, "I have no money!"

"Give up your money, or we'll kill you!" said the second figure, in a voice Pinocchio had heard somewhere else.

The puppet opened his mouth to plead for his life. As he did so the coins beneath his tongue chinked.

"So you've hidden your money in your mouth!" cried the taller of the two figures. "Spit it out!"

Pinocchio shook his head stubbornly. The second figure took out a knife and tried to force it between the puppet's lips. Pinocchio suddenly opened his mouth and bit off the figure's hand. He spat it out. To his surprise he saw that it was the paw of a cat that was lying on the ground.

The cat screamed. Pinocchio jumped over a hedge and ran for his life. His two attackers raced after him, although the cat who had lost a paw was forced to hobble badly.

They ran for what seemed a long time through the dark. Pinocchio could not shake the other two off. Finally in desperation, he climbed a tall pine tree and perched in its topmost branches. The two figures clad in sacks tried to climb after him, but kept slipping back down again. Then they lit a fire at the base of the tree and kept throwing dry sticks on to it. Soon the tree was blazing fiercely. Pinocchio jumped down and set off across the fields again. His two attackers kept doggedly after him.

Dawn was beginning to break when Pinocchio stumbled across a wide ditch full of dirty water. He hesitated. What could he do? Another minute and the other two would be upon him. The puppet braced himself.

"One, two, three!" he cried, and with a great effort cleared the ditch.

He turned and looked back. His pursuers were dithering on the far side of the ditch. As Pinocchio stared at them they made up their minds. Both sack-clad figures dashed at the water and tried to leap across the ditch. Each fell short and descended into the water with a splash! Pinocchio laughed.

"Enjoy your bath!" he shouted, and trotted off.

Soon it was daylight. Pinocchio slowed down to a walk. He began to pass people as he strolled across the fields. He was safe enough now. He made his way to a road and walked along it.

As he was passing a big oak tree, he heard someone moving in the bushes at the side of the road. Pinocchio stopped. After a moment the fox and the cat appeared. Both looked very clean, as if they had had a good wash.

"Dear Pinocchio," shouted the fox, kissing the puppet. "What are you doing here?"

"Oh, it's a long story," said Pinocchio. "Early this morning I was attacked by two robbers. They wanted to take my gold coins from me."

"Never!" exclaimed the cat. "Aren't some people wicked!"

"Anyway, I managed to escape, so that's all right," said the puppet. Suddenly he saw that the cat seemed lame, with one paw missing. "What happened to your paw?" he asked.

The cat looked confused, but the fox answered quickly. "Dear old cat," he said fondly, "she's so generous. Give anyone anything, she will. Why, back down the road we met an old wolf, starving to death. Quick as you like, my friend here bit off her paw and gave it to the poor fellow for breakfast. She's like that, she is."

"Never mind that," growled the cat. "It's lucky we met you, Pinocchio. The Field of Miracles isn't very far away. We can be there in half an hour. Come on!"

The three of them walked on down the road. Before long they came to a town.

49

"What do they call this place?" asked the puppet curiously.

"Er, Fools' Trap," said the fox. "I can't think why," he added.

Pinocchio glanced from side to side as they walked through the streets of the town. It really did seem a most unusual place. Almost everyone in it seemed to be suffering in some way. The dogs had lost their coats and the sheep their fleeces, and were shivering with the cold. Butterflies had sold their wings and were walking; peacocks were without their tails, and pheasants had lost their lovely feathers.

The only inhabitants who seemed to be happy were a few foxes being driven past in great coaches, and a magpie or two being carried by footmen through the streets.

The lame fox and the blind cat took Pinocchio through the town, and out of its boundaries to a field. It seemed just like every other field that the puppet had ever seen.

"Here we are," said the cat impatiently. "This is the Field of Miracles. Dig a small hole with your hands and put your four gold coins in it."

Pinocchio did as he was told. He dug the hole, put in the gold pieces, and covered them over with earth.

"Now you must bring some water from the special stream over there," said the fox, "and sprinkle it over the earth."

Pinocchio carried the water in his shoe from the stream and poured it over the hole he had dug.

"What should I do next?" he asked when he had finished.

"That's all," said the fox. "Now we must all go away. If you come back on your own in about twenty minutes, you will find four trees bearing many gold coins growing where you have dug your hole. No, no, we want no thanks. It has been a pleasure to know you, Pinocchio."

The fox and the cat went off in one direction, while Pinocchio wandered off the other way, back into the city. Soon he was out of sight of the field. His mind was full of great fancies as he tried to make up his mind what he would buy with his new wealth. Only when he was quite sure that twenty minutes had passed did the puppet turn and make his way back to the Field of Miracles.

To his amazement there were no trees growing where he had planted his four gold pieces. Pinocchio waited impatiently, in case he had come back too soon. Still nothing happened. With a sinking heart the puppet realised that something had gone wrong. Wondering what had caused the delay he started to dig up the earth. There was no sign of his money. He dug deeper and harder. Still there was nothing there, not even his four gold coins.

A great screech of laughter came from a tree above him. The puppet glared up to see an old parrot cleaning the few feathers it had left.

"What are you laughing at?" demanded Pinocchio, trembling with anxiety.

"I am laughing because you have been cheated," answered the parrot boldly, "just as I was cheated when first I came to Fools' Trap."

"Cheated?" asked Pinocchio in dismay. "How have I been cheated?"

"While you were away," chuckled the parrot, "the fox and the cat came back and dug up your four gold pieces. They will be far away by now, and you will never catch them up."

Pinocchio turned back to the hole at his feet. He dug deeper and deeper and deeper. Soon there was a great cavern yawning at his feet, but no gold pieces.

The puppet climbed back up to the field and ran off to the town as fast as his legs would carry him.

There he lost no time reporting to the judge in the court house that he had been cheated out of his money. The judge listened kindly to all that the puppet had to tell him. When Pinocchio had finished his sorry tale the judge rang a bell at his side.

At once two great mastiffs dressed as policemen appeared in the doorway.

"Another poor fool complaining," said the judge in a bored tone.

"Take him to prison at once."

Pinocchio tried to protest, but the great dogs put their paws under his arms and dragged him off to the cells.

For four long months the puppet remained in prison. Then he had a stroke of luck. The King of Fools' Trap won a great battle. To celebrate, he ordered that all the rascals in the town's prison be set free.

One by one the other prisoners were released until only the puppet remained in the cells.

"Why haven't I been allowed to go, too?" asked Pinocchio.

"I'm afraid that only rascals are to be set free," said the jailer. "You claim to be an honest fellow."

"No, no, I'm a rascal, I'm a rascal!" cried Pinocchio quickly.

"In that case," said the jailer, bowing low, "please permit me to escort you from the prison."

Once he was out of the cells, Pinocchio ran and ran until the town of Fools' Trap was far behind him. It began to rain and soon the road was very muddy, but still the puppet did not slow down.

"What a fool I've been," said Pinocchio to himself, as he hurried down the road. "I've deserved everything that's happened to me. I've been as obstinate as a mule, I've been selfish, and I've never listened to good advice. But that's all behind me now. If only I'm allowed to reach home safely, I'll be a different puppet. I'll be good, obedient and loving, I promise I will!"

The words were hardly out of his mouth when he stopped and jumped back in fright. Stretched across the road in front of him was a great serpent. Its skin was green, its eyes were red and from its tail poured clouds of smoke.

Pinocchio waited, hoping that the serpent would move on, but the great beast stayed where it was. In the end the puppet summoned up his courage and walked towards it.

"Excuse me, sir," he said respectfully, "I would like to go home. It's been such a long time since I was there. Do you think you could move just a little, so that I could pass?"

The serpent did not answer. Pinocchio thought perhaps it was asleep. He walked back a little and then ran forward to leap over the great beast. Just as he did so the serpent raised its head to strike the puppet. In his fright Pinocchio overbalanced and fell backwards. His head got stuck in the mud and his legs waved wildly in the air.

The sight of Pinocchio looking so ridiculous made the serpent laugh so heartily that it could not strike at the puppet. Instead it laughed and laughed so much that suddenly it choked. At the same time a blood vessel burst in its heart, killing the serpent.

Pinocchio climbed over the dead body and set off running towards his home.

"Perhaps my luck is beginning to change for the better," he said as he went.

THE WATER BABIES

by Charles Kingsley

Although he was only a boy, Tom had been a chimney sweep. He had the hard and dangerous job of climbing up narrow chimneys with his brushes. Then he was changed. A fairy turned him into a water-baby, just a few centimetres long, who could spend all his time swimming at the bottom of rivers.

Tom loved his new life in the water. Sometimes he went along the smooth gravel waterways, looking at the crickets which ran in and out among the pebbles. Then he would swim into the great water forests. There were water flowers there in their thousands. Tom tried to pick them: but as soon as he touched them, they drew themselves in and turned into knots of jelly; and then Tom saw that they were all alive—bells, and stars, and wheels of all shapes and colours.

The water-baby soon learned the language of the creatures living in the water, and was able to talk to them. One day he came across a great ugly creature sitting just under the bank of the river. It was about half as big as himself, with six legs and a great stomach, and a most ridiculous head with two great eyes and a face just like a donkey's.

"Oh," said Tom, "you are an ugly fellow, to be sure!" and he began making faces at him.

Suddenly a long arm with a pair of pincers on the end shot out and caught Tom by the nose. It did not hurt him much; but held him quite tight.

"Yah, ah! Oh, let me go!" cried Tom.

"Then leave me alone," said the creature. "I want to split."

"Why do you want to split?" asked Tom, rubbing his nose when it was released.

"Because my brothers and my sisters have all split, and turned into beautiful creatures with wings; and I want to split too. Don't speak to me. I am sure I shall split. I will split!"

Tom stood still and watched him. And the creature swelled himself, and puffed, and stretched himself out stiff, and at last—crack, puff, bang—he opened up all down his back, and then up to the top of his head.

And out of his inside came the most slender, elegant, soft creature as soft and smooth as Tom: but very pale and weak, like a little child who had been ill a long time in a dark room. Then it began walking slowly up a grass stem to the top of the water.

Tom was so astonished that he said not a word: but he stared wide-eyed. Then he went up to the top of the water too, and peeped out to see what would happen.

As the creature sat in the warm sun, a wonderful change came over it. It grew strong and firm; the most lovely colours began to show on its body, blue, yellow, black, and spots, bars and rings. Out of its back rose four great wings of bright brown gauze. Its eyes grew so large that they filled all its head, and shone like ten thousand diamonds.

"Oh, you beautiful creature!" said Tom; and he put out his hand to catch it.

But the thing whirled up into the air, and hung poised on its wings for a moment, and looked down at Tom.

"No," it said, "you cannot catch me. I am a dragon-fly now, the king of all the flies. I shall dance in the sunshine, catch gnats, and have a beautiful wife like myself. Goodbye!"

Tom watched the dragon-fly fluttering over the river until it disappeared from sight. Then he dived back down to the bottom. He found himself in the middle of a shoal of trout, and swam along with them. As they leapt out of the water to catch flies, so Tom jumped too.

Presently it came on to rain. Then the thunder roared, and the lightning flashed, till the rocks in the stream seemed to shake. Tom looked up at the storm above through the water, and thought it the finest thing he had ever seen in his life.

The rain poured into the river, causing it to rise higher and higher and rush along at a great rate, full of beetles, sticks, straws, worms, wood-lice and leeches.

Tom could hardly stand against the power of the stream, and hid behind a rock. But the trout did not. Out they rushed from among the stones and began gobbling the beetles and leeches.

By flashes of lightning, Tom saw a great new sight—all the bottom of the river alive with great eels, turning and twisting along and away. They had been hiding for weeks past in the cracks of the rocks. As they hurried past Tom could hear them say to each other, "We must run, we must run. What a jolly thunderstorm! Down to the sea, down to the sea!"

Then the otter came by with all her brood, sweeping along as fast as the eels themselves. She spied Tom as she came by, and said: "Now is your time, if you want to see the world. Come along, children, never mind those nasty eels. We shall breakfast on salmon tomorrow. Down to the sea, down to the sea!"

Tom needed no more invitation. He followed the others in the great rush to the sea. On and on he went in that great floating procession; on through narrow passages and great roaring waterfalls; past sleeping villages and under great bridges, away and away to the sea. And when daylight came, he was there, at the mouth of the great river where it joined the ocean. Tom felt a little frightened.

"What a great wide place it is," he said to himself. "If I go into it I shall surely lose my way."

So he went back a little way and slept in the crack of a rock. When he awoke it was light and the river was calm again as it flowed into the great sea. Then Tom saw a sight which made him jump up.

Such a fish! ten times as big as the biggest trout, and a hundred times as big as Tom, sculling up the river. It was shining silver from head to tail, with here and there a crimson dot; a grand hooked nose and a curling lip. As Tom looked on, it leapt high out of the water and over a rock. The water-baby knew that this must be a salmon, the king of fish.

Slowly and carefully Tom swam out into the wide sea. He passed shoals of bass and mullet, leaping and rushing after shrimps; and once he passed a huge shining seal.

"How do you do, sir?" piped Tom. "What a beautiful place the sea is!"

Instead of trying to bite him, the seal looked at Tom with his soft, sleepy, winking eyes, and said, "Good tide to you, my little man!"

Tom went on, calling out cheerful greetings to fleets of purple sea-snails and a shoal of porpoises, all smooth and shining as if they had been polished. Then he swam in towards the shore, and before long he was among the rocks in the shallow water off the beach. He chatted idly to the barnacles clinging to the rocks, and then turned a corner. Suddenly he saw a sort of cage ahead of him. Inside it was a sad-looking lobster, twiddling with his horns instead of thumbs.

"Hello," said Tom. "Have you been naughty and been put in a lock-up?"

"I can't get out," groaned the lobster.

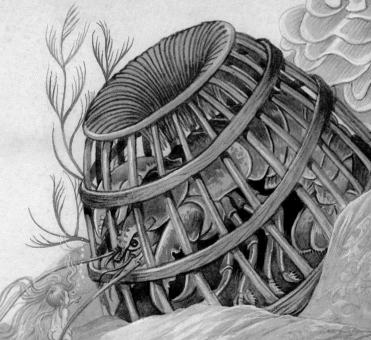

"The point is," said Tom, "how did you get in there in the first place?"

"Don't you know what this is?" demanded the lobster. "This is a lobster-pot, left among the rocks by fishermen to catch creatures like me. Before long, a man will come by, open the pot, and take me home for his supper."

"Oh dear," said Tom thoughtfully. "We can't have that."

"I just can't get out," said the lobster. "I've jumped upwards, downwards, backwards, and sideways at least four thousand times; I always end up back here. I can't find the hole I came in through. There are great spikes in here, so if I move about too much, I'll tear myself on them."

Tom looked at the trap carefully, and thought he saw a way of freeing the prisoner.

"Turn your tail up to me," he said, "and I'll pull you through, and you won't stick on the spikes."

But the lobster was so stupid and clumsy that he couldn't reach the hole. Tom reached down till he grasped the lobster. Then the clumsy creature pulled him into the trap head-first.

"This is a pretty fix!" said the water-baby. "Never mind, I can see a way out. Take your great claws and break the points of these spikes. Then we can get up to the hole and go out through it."

"Dear me," said the lobster, "I never thought of that."

In no time at all he had broken off the spikes in the lobster pot. The lobster and Tom swam out through the hole and made their escape hastily.

"Much obliged," nodded the lobster, hurrying off across the rocks. "I hope I can do you a favour some time."

"Think nothing of it," called out Tom, and he dived back into the water.

THE COWARDLY LION

by Frank Baum

Dorothy had been an ordinary girl living on a farm in Kansas in the USA. In a great storm she had been knocked senseless.

When she came round she found that she was no longer on the farm. Instead she was in the strange land of Oz. A Good Witch told her that if she wanted to get back home to Kansas again, she would have to follow the yellow brick road to the Emerald City, where she would find the marvellous Wizard of Oz.

The brave girl set out on her long journey, her little dog Toto by her side. On the way, Dorothy made two friends who decided to go with her to see the Wizard. The stuffed Scarecrow thought that he would ask the Wizard for some brains, while the Tin Woodman, who was always getting rusty, said that he would ask the Wizard for a heart.

They walked through thick woods. The road was still paved with yellow bricks, but these were almost covered with dried branches and dead leaves, and the walking was not at all good.

There were few birds in this part of the forest, for birds love the open country where there is plenty of sunshine. But now and then there came a deep growl from some wild animal hidden among the trees. These sounds made the little girl's heart beat fast, for she did not know what made them; but Toto knew, and he walked close to Dorothy's side, and did not even bark in return.

"How long will it be?" the child asked of the Tin Woodman, "before we are out of the forest?"

"I cannot tell," was the answer, "for I have never been to the Emerald City. My father told me once that it was a long journey through dangerous countryside."

Just as he spoke there came from the forest a terrible roar, and the next moment a great Lion bounded into the road. With one blow of his paw he sent the Scarecrow spinning over and over to the edge of the road, and then he struck at the Tin Woodman with his sharp claws. But, to the Lion's surprise, he could make no impression on the tin, although the Woodman fell over in the road and lay still.

Little Toto, now that he had an enemy to face, ran barking towards the Lion, and the great beast opened his mouth to bite the dog, but Dorothy, fearing Toto would be killed, rushed forward and slapped the Lion upon his nose as hard as she could, while she cried out:

"Don't you dare to bite Toto! You ought to be ashamed of yourself, a big beast like you, to bite a poor little dog!"

"I didn't bite him," said the Lion, as he rubbed his nose with his paw where Dorothy had hit it.

"No, but you tried to," she said sharply. "You are nothing but a big coward."

"I know it," said the Lion, hanging his head in shame. "I've always known it. But how can I help it?"

"I don't know, I'm sure. To think of your striking a stuffed man, like the poor Scarecrow!"

"Is he stuffed?" asked the Lion in surprise, while he watched her pick up the Scarecrow, set him upon his feet, and pat him into shape again.

"Of course he's stuffed," replied Dorothy, who was still angry.

"That's why he went over so easily," remarked the Lion. "It astonished me to see him whirl around so. Is the other one stuffed also?"

"No," said Dorothy, "he's made of tin." She helped the Woodman up again.

"That's why he nearly blunted my claws," said the Lion. "When they scratched against the tin it made a cold shiver run down my back. What is that little animal you are so careful of?"

"He is my dog, Toto."

"Is he made of tin, or stuffed?"

"Neither. He's a—a—a meat dog," said the girl.

"Oh! He's a curious animal and now that I look at him, seems remarkably small. No one would think of biting such a little thing except a coward like me," said the Lion sadly.

"What makes you a coward?" asked Dorothy, looking at the great beast in wonder, for he was as big as a small horse.

"It is a mystery," replied the Lion. "I suppose I was born that way. All the other animals in the forest naturally expect me to be brave, for the Lion is thought to be the King of the Beasts. I learned that if I roared very loudly every living thing was frightened and got out of my way. Whenever I've met a man, I've been scared. But I've just roared at him, and he has always ran away as fast as he could go. But really I'm very frightened myself."

"Most peculiar," said Dorothy.

"Anyway, where are you all going?" asked the Lion.

"I'm going to the Wizard of Oz to ask for some brains, for my head is stuffed with straw," said the Scarecrow.

"And I'm going to ask him to give me a heart," said the Tin Woodman.

"And I'm going to ask him to send Toto and me back to Kansas," said Dorothy.

"Then if you don't mind," said the Lion, "I'll come with you and ask the Wizard to give me some courage."

"You will be very welcome," said Dorothy.

So once more the little company set off upon the journey, the Lion walking with stately strides at the girl's side. For a time it was a quiet journey, marred only when the Tin Woodman stepped upon a beetle. This upset the Woodman and made him cry. The tears ran slowly down his face and over the hinges of his jaw, and there they rusted. When Dorothy asked him a question, the Tin Woodman could not open his mouth, for his jaws were rusted together. The Scarecrow seized the oil-can from Dorothy's basket and oiled the Woodman's jaws, so that after a few moments he could talk as well as before.

"That will teach me to look where I step," he said. "For if I should kill another bug or beetle I should surely cry again, and crying rusts my jaws so that I cannot speak."

Before long they came across a great ditch that crossed the road and divided the forest as far as they could see on either side. It was a very wide ditch, and when they crept up to the edge and looked into it they could see that it was also very deep, and there were many big, jagged rocks at the bottom. The sides were so steep that none of them could climb down. For a moment it seemed that their journey must end.

"What shall we do?" asked Dorothy in despair.

"I think I could jump over it," said the Lion slowly.

"Then we are all right," said the Scarecrow, "for you can carry us all over on your back, one at a time."

"Well, I'll try it," said the Lion. "Who will go first?"

"I will," declared the Scarecrow, "for, if you found that you could not jump over the gulf, Dorothy would be killed, or the Tin Woodman badly dented on the rocks below. But if I am on your back it will not matter so much, for the fall would not hurt me at all."

"I am terribly afraid myself of falling," said the Cowardly Lion, "but I suppose there is nothing to do but try it. Get on my back."

The Scarecrow sat on the Lion's back. The big beast walked to the edge of the ditch and crouched down. Then giving a great spring, he shot through the air and landed safely on the other side. They were all greatly pleased to see how easily he did it, and after the Scarecrow had got down from his back, the Lion sprang across the ditch again.

Dorothy thought she would go next. So she took Toto in her arms and climbed on the Lion's back, holding tightly to his mane with one hand. The next moment it seemed as if she were flying through the air; and then, before she had time to think about it, she was safe on the other side. The Lion went back a third time and got the Tin Woodman, and then they all sat down for a while to give the beast a rest.

They found the forest very thick on this side, and it looked dark and gloomy. After the Lion had rested they started along the road of yellow brick, silently wondering, each in his own mind, if ever they would come to the end of the woods and reach the bright sunshine again. To add to their discomfort, they soon heard strange noises in the depths of the forest, and the Lion whispered to them that it was in this part of the country that the Kalidahs lived.

"What are Kalidahs?" asked the girl.

"They are monstrous beasts with bodies like bears and heads like tigers," replied the Lion, "and with claws so long and sharp that they could tear me in two as easily as I could kill Toto. I'm terribly afraid of the Kalidahs."

"I'm not surprised that you are," agreed Dorothy. "They must be dreadful beasts."

The Lion was about to reply, when suddenly they came to another gulf across the road. But this one was so broad and deep that the Lion knew at once he could not leap across it.

So they sat down to consider what they should do. After serious thought the Scarecrow said, "Here is a great tree, standing close to the ditch. If the Tin Woodman can chop it down, so that it will fall to the other side, we can walk across it easily."

"That is a first-rate idea," said the Lion. "One would almost suspect you had brains in your head, instead of straw."

The Woodman set to work at once, and so sharp was his axe that the tree was soon nearly chopped through. Then the Lion put his strong front legs against the tree and pushed with all his might. Slowly the big tree tipped and fell with a crash across the ditch, with its top branches on the other side.

They had just started to cross this queer bridge when a sharp growl made them all look up. To their horror they saw running toward them two great beasts with bodies like bears and heads like tigers.

"They are the Kalidahs!" said the Cowardly Lion, beginning to tremble.

"Quick!" cried the Scarecrow. "Let us cross over."

So Dorothy went first, holding Toto in her arms. The Tin Woodman followed, and the Scarecrow came next. The Lion, although he was certainly afraid, turned to face the Kalidahs. Then he gave so loud and terrible a roar that Dorothy screamed and the Scarecrow fell over backward. Even the fierce beasts stopped short and looked at him in surprise.

But, seeing that they were bigger than the Lion, and remembering that there were two of them and only one of him, the Kalidahs again rushed forward. The Lion crossed over the tree and turned to see what they would do next. Without stopping an instant the fierce beasts also began to cross the tree. And the Lion said to Dorothy, "We are lost, for they will surely tear us to pieces with their sharp claws. But stand close behind me, and I will fight them as long as I am alive."

"Wait a minute!" called the Scarecrow. He had been thinking what was best to be done. Now he asked the Woodman to chop away the end of the tree that rested on their side of the ditch. The Tin Woodman began to use his axe at once. Just as the two Kalidahs were nearly across, the tree fell with a crash into the gulf, carrying the ugly, snarling brutes with it, and both were dashed to pieces on the sharp rocks at the bottom.

"Well," said the Cowardly Lion, drawing a long breath of relief. "I see we are going to live a little while longer."

The little group hurried on. Towards the end of the afternoon the trees became thinner, and they suddenly came upon a broad river, flowing swiftly just before them. On the other side of the water they could see the road of yellow brick running through a beautiful country, with green fields dotted with bright flowers and all the road bordered with trees hanging full of delicious fruits.

"How shall we cross the river?" Dorothy asked.

"The Tin Woodman must build us a raft, so that we may float to the other side," said the Scarecrow.

So the Woodman took his axe and began to chop down small trees to make a raft, while Dorothy found a pleasant spot under a tree and sat down and closed her eyes. Soon she was dreaming of the Emerald City, and of the Wizard of Oz, who would soon send her back to her own home again.

THE HAPPY PRINCE

by Oscar Wilde

High above the city, on a tall column, stood the statue of the Happy Prince. He was gilded all over with thin leaves of fine gold, for eyes he had two bright sapphires, and a large red ruby glowed on his sword-hilt.

One night there flew over the city a little Swallow. His friends had flown south to the warm lands six weeks before, but he was late and was hurrying to get away before it grew too cold.

He saw the statue on the tall column and decided to spend the night in its shelter. He was about to go to sleep between the statue's feet when a large drop of water fell on him.

The bird looked up and saw that the eyes of the Happy Prince were filled with tears. They were running down his golden cheeks and falling to the ground.

"Why are you crying?" asked the Swallow.

"It is because I can see all the ugliness and misery of the city from up here," said the statue. "Although my heart is only made of lead, I must weep."

"What can you see that makes you so sad?" asked the bird.

"In a little street," said the Prince, "there is a poor house. One of the windows is open. I can see a woman sitting at a table. She is poor and hungry. In a bed in a corner of the room her little boy is lying ill. He has a fever, and he is asking for oranges. His mother has nothing to give him but river-water. Swallow, will you take her the ruby from my sword-hilt? She can sell it and buy food. My feet are fixed to the ground, so I cannot go myself."

"My friends are waiting for me in the warm lands," said the Swallow.

"Stay one night and be my messenger," begged the Happy Prince.

The statue looked so sad that the little Swallow was sorry. "It is very cold here," he said, "but I will stay with you for one night, and be your messenger."

"Thank you, little Swallow," said the Prince.

So the bird picked out the great ruby from the Prince's sword, and flew away with it in his beak over the roofs of the town. At last he

came to the poor house and looked in. The boy was lying on his bed, and his mother had fallen asleep, she was so tired.

In hopped the bird, and laid the great ruby on the table by the woman's head. Then he flew gently round the room, fanning the boy's forehead with his wings. "How cool I feel," said the boy. "I must be getting better," and he sank into a deep sleep.

Then the Swallow flew back to the Happy Prince, and told him what he had done.

"It is curious," he remarked, "but I feel quite warm now, although it is so cold."

"That is because you have done a good deed," said the statue. And the little Swallow began to think, and then he fell asleep. Thinking always made him sleepy.

When day broke, he flew down to the river and had a bath. Then he went back to the Happy Prince.

"I am just off to the warm lands," he chirped.

"Swallow, Swallow, little Swallow," said the statue, "will you not stay with me one night longer?"

"My friends are waiting for me in the warm lands," said the bird.

"Swallow," said the Happy Prince, "far away across the city I see a young man in a tiny room. He is leaning over a desk covered with papers. He is trying to finish writing a play, but he is too cold to write any more. There is no fire in the grate, and hunger has made him faint." 67

"I will wait with you one night longer," said the Swallow, who really had a good heart. "Shall I take him another ruby?"

"Alas! I have no ruby now," said the Prince. "My eyes are all I have left. Pluck one of them out and take it to him. He will sell it, and buy firewood, and finish his play."

"Dear Prince," said the Swallow, "I cannot do that," and he began to weep.

"Swallow, Swallow, little Swallow," said the Happy Prince, "do as I ask you."

So the Swallow plucked out the Prince's eye, and flew away to the writer's room. It was easy enough to get in, as there was a hole in the roof. Through this he darted, and came into the room. The young man had his head buried in his hands, so he did not hear the flutter of the bird's wings. When he looked up he found the beautiful jewel at his side.

"This must be from some great admirer!" he cried. "Now I can finish my play!"

The next day the Swallow flew down to the harbour. He sat on the mast of a large vessel and watched the sailors. "I am going to the warm lands," he cried, but nobody minded, and when the moon rose he flew back to the Happy Prince.

"I have come to say goodbye," he cried.

"Swallow, Swallow, little Swallow," said the Prince, "will you not stay with me one night longer?"

"It is winter," replied the bird, "and the chill snow will soon be here. I must leave you, but I will never forget you."

"In the square below," said the Happy Prince, "there is a little girl selling matches. She has let her matches fall in the gutter, and they are all spoiled. Her father will beat her if she does not bring home some money, and she is crying. She has no shoes or stockings, and her little head is bare. Pluck out my other eye, and give it to her, and her father will not beat her."

"I will stay with you one night longer," said the Swallow, "but I cannot pluck out your eye. You would be quite blind then."

"Swallow, Swallow, little Swallow," said the Prince, "do as I ask you."

So he took out the statue's other eye, and darted down with it. He swooped past the match-girl, and slipped the jewel into the palm of her hand. "What a lovely bit of glass," said the little girl; and she ran home laughing.

Then the Swallow came back to the Happy Prince. "You are blind now," he said, "so I will stay with you always."

"No, little Swallow," said the Prince, "you must go away to the warm lands."

"I will stay with you always," said the Swallow, and he slept at the Happy Prince's feet.

All the next day he sat on the Prince's shoulder, and told him stories of what he had seen in strange lands. He told him of the red birds who catch fish in their beaks; of the great green snake that sleeps in a palm tree, and has twenty priests to feed it with honey-cakes; and of the little folk who sail over a big lake on large flat leaves, and are always at war with the butterflies.

"Dear little Swallow," said the Prince, "you tell me of amazing things, but more amazing than anything is the suffering of men and women. Fly over my city, little Swallow, and tell me what you see there."

So the Swallow flew over the great city, and saw the rich making merry in their great houses, while the beggars were sitting at their gates. He flew into dark lanes and saw the white faces of starving children looking out at the black streets.

Under the archway of a bridge two little boys were lying in one another's arms, to try and keep themselves warm. "How hungry we are!" they said. "You must not lie here!" shouted the watchman, and they walked out into the rain.

Then the Swallow flew back and told the Prince what he had seen.

"I am covered with fine gold," said the statue, "you must take it off, leaf by leaf, and give it to my poor; the living always think that gold can make them happy."

Leaf after leaf of fine gold the Swallow picked off, till the Happy Prince looked quite dull and grey. Leaf after leaf of fine gold he brought to the poor, and the children's faces grew rosier; and they laughed and played games in the street.

"We have bread now!" they laughed.

Then the snow came, and after the snow came the frost. The streets looked as if they were made of silver, they were so bright and glistening. Everybody went about in furs, and the little boys wore scarlet caps and skated on the ice.

The poor little Swallow grew colder and colder, but he would not leave the Prince; he loved him so well. He picked up crumbs outside the baker's door when the baker was not looking, and tried to keep himself warm by flapping his wings.

But at last he knew that he was going to die. He had just enough strength to fly up to the Prince's shoulder once more. "Goodbye, dear Prince," he murmured, "will you let me kiss your hand."

"I am glad that you are going to the warm lands at last, little Swallow," said the Prince, "you have stayed here too long; but you must kiss me on the lips, for I love you."

"It is not to the warm lands that I am going," said the Swallow. "I am going to the House of Death. Death is the Brother of Sleep, is he not?"

And he kissed the Happy Prince on the lips, and fell down dead at his feet.

At that moment a curious crack sounded inside the statue, as if something had broken. The fact is that the leaden heart had snapped right in two. It certainly was a dreadfully hard frost.

Early next morning the Mayor was walking in the square below with the Town Councillors. As they passed the column he looked up at the statue. "Dear me! how shabby the Happy Prince looks!" he said.

"How shabby indeed!" cried the Town Councillors, who always agreed with the Mayor; and they went up to look at it.

"The ruby has fallen out of his sword, his eyes are gone, and he is golden no longer," said the Mayor; "in fact he is little better than a beggar!"

"Little better than a beggar!" said the Town Councillors.

"And here is a dead bird at our feet," said the Mayor. "Birds should not be allowed to die here."

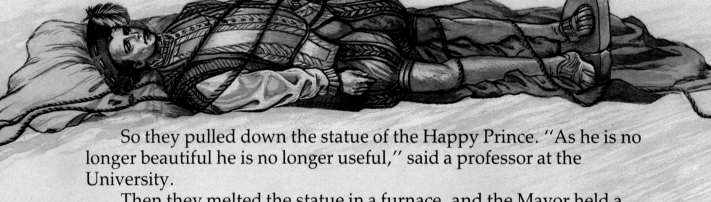

So they pulled down the statue of the Happy Prince. "As he is no longer beautiful he is no longer useful," said a professor at the University.

Then they melted the statue in a furnace, and the Mayor held a meeting of the Councillors to decide what was to be done with the metal. "We must have another statue, of course," he said, "and it shall be a statue of myself."

"Of myself," said each of the Town Councillors, and they quarrelled. When I last heard of them they were quarrelling still.

"What a strange thing," said the foreman in charge of the workmen at the furnace. "The broken lead heart will not melt in the heat. We must throw it away." So they threw it on a dust-heap where the dead Swallow was also lying.

"Bring me the two most precious things in the city," said God to one of his Angels; and the Angel brought Him the leaden heart and the dead bird.

"You have rightly chosen," said God, "for in my garden of Paradise this little bird shall sing for evermore, and in my city of gold the Happy Prince shall praise me."

THE TRAVELS OF BARON MUNCHAUSEN

by Rudolph Raspe

There are some who say that I exaggerate too much and that the tales of my life cannot be believed. I say in return that my life has been so exciting that I have had adventures beyond the belief of those who stay at home. Many of these great doings seem to have been concerned with animals.

When I was still a young man I visited the island of Ceylon and went out on a shooting expedition. Near the banks of a large piece of water I heard a rustling noise behind me. I turned to see a lion advancing upon me. My musket was filled only with pellets for shooting birds, and would have no effect on this beast. I was sure that my end had come.

I turned to flee. The moment I turned about I saw a large crocodile coming out of the water towards me, his mouth wide open.

I fell to the ground in fear. At that very moment the lion sprang at me. I lay expecting at any moment to feel his teeth tearing at me. Nothing happened. I raised my head. To my great joy I saw that the lion had soared right over my form and had dived down the throat of the waiting crocodile. The latter half of his body was sticking out of the crocodile's mouth. As I watched, the lion suffocated and the crocodile choked to death. When my companions found me I was standing proudly over the two dead bodies.

Some years later I was travelling in the frozen land of Russia in the middle of a dreadful winter. On my way across the snows I passed what I took to be a poor peasant lying on the ground, freezing to death. I took pity on the poor fellow and dropped my cloak over him before riding on. As I did so, I heard the man's voice calling after me,

"You will be given a great reward for this kindness!"

I rode on until night fell, meeting no one else on my journey. I became very tired and dismounted to sleep. In front of me, sticking out of the snow, was something like the pointed stump of a tree. I tied the reins of my horse to this to prevent him from wandering away in the night. Then I fell asleep.

The next morning, when I woke up, I found that I was lying on the ground in a churchyard on the edge of a village. I could see my horse nowhere. Then I heard him neigh above my head. I looked upwards. There he was, hanging by his reins from the steeple of the church!

I realised what had happened. The whole village had been covered with snow to a great depth in the storm the previous day. The snow had been piled so high that it had almost covered the church steeple, all except the tiny part which I had seen and to which I had tied my mount.

During the night, while I had been sleeping so soundly, much of the snow beneath me had melted, carrying me gently down to the ground. My poor horse, on the other hand, had remained tied to the steeple.

Fortunately getting the mount down presented no problem. I picked up one of my pistols, took aim and fired. My shot broke the reins and the horse fell to earth, landing in a pile of soft snow. I repaired the reins, mounted and rode off.

My poor horse had escaped this time, but it was not long before he met his end. The snow underfoot had become so thick that I had tied a sledge to my horse and was being dragged along on this sledge by my mount through a dreadful forest. Suddenly a large wolf leapt out of the trees and gave chase. My horse pulled me away on the sledge as fast as he could, but it was not long before the wolf caught up with us. He leapt clean over the sledge and fell upon the hind-quarters of my horse, starting to swallow and eat my mount.

I raised my head and saw to my horror what was happening. In an effort to help the horse I started hitting the wolf with my whip. This unexpected attack from the rear so frightened the wolf that he leapt forward with all his might. The carcase of the dead horse fell to the ground, but by this time the wolf was caught up in the harness, and could not free himself. He was now pulling the sledge instead of the horse, and by using my reins and my whip I was able to control him until we reached the next town, where I shot the wolf and bought a new horse.

In order to obtain food on my travels I depended a great deal on my skill as a hunter, and some of my expeditions in the large forests in search of food were responsible for one or two incredible adventures.

Once I came across a great wild boar, with two enormous curved tusks. I fired and missed. There was no time to reload, so I ran and hid behind a tree. Almost blind with rage the boar charged at the tree concealing me. He hit it with a tremendous shock, and his tusks became embedded deep in the trunk of the tree, holding him fast.

Cautiously I emerged from my hiding place. The boar struggled and squealed, but he was held fast by his own sharp tusks. I picked up a large stone and hammered away at those tusks until they were so bent that there was no possible chance of the boar releasing himself from the tree. Then I went off to fetch a horse and cart with which to pick up my prisoner.

It was in the same vast forest that I had my strange encounter with a stag. He was a noble beast, with great antlers growing out of his head. I raised my musket to fire at him, and then realised that I had used up all my ammunition, leaving only a small supply of powder.

Then I remembered that for my lunch I had eaten a handful of cherries. Not wishing to litter the ground with my rubbish I had placed the stones in my pocket. I took these out now and put them in my musket, along with the gunpowder. Taking careful aim I fired the stones at the stag. As usual my aim was perfect.

The cherry stones struck the beast in the centre of the forehead with tremendous force, almost stunning him. Somehow the stag managed to stagger off among the trees and escape.

A year later I was hunting with some friends in that same part of the forest. Out came the stag I had fired at twelve months before. I recognised him at once, for growing out of the middle of his forehead, where my cherry stones had struck him, was a fine cherry tree. I shot the beast, skinned it, cooked the meat and ate it with some cherry sauce made from the tree that had been growing out of its head.

In the course of my life I had some strange experiences with tame animals as well as with wild ones. Once, I remember, I owned a greyhound. This was the swiftest dog I ever knew, and he never lost a race. Unfortunately in these races he ran so fast that over the years he quite wore down his legs, until in the end they were no longer than those of a dachshund. Naturally I had to retire the animal as a racing dog, and keep him as a pet, and for many years more he would scurry around after me on his tiny legs.

My favourite horse Ajax also had his share of marvellous adventures. Once I rode him into battle against the Turks when I was in command of a fine body of soldiers. One day we came across a body of mounted Turks and attacked them so bravely that the Turks and their horses soon turned and fled. Of course my men and I rode after them as fast as we could go. Ajax was much faster than any other horse in my command, and we soon out-distanced the rest of my soldiers, so that I was chasing those Turks on my own.

I followed them until they reached their fortress, and even went in after them when their guards raised the portcullis, the gate with the huge sharp spikes in the fortress wall.

Once I was in the yard of the fortress, however, I realised that I was on my own, and that even I could not defeat the entire Turkish force without the aid of my soldiers. I at once turned Ajax and rode out of the yard. As I did so, the Turks brought the portcullis down hard behind me in an attempt to trap me.

I rode back swiftly until I reached the nearest friendly town. There I decided to wait until the rest of my men caught up with me. In the meantime, I decided Ajax must be thirsty after all his hard riding, so I rode him over to a pond in the town square, remaining on his back while he drank his fill.

That poor beast drank and drank until the pond was drained. I was amazed. Then I heard the sound of water running away behind me. I turned in my saddle and gazed back. To my astonishment I saw that the entire rear part of the horse had been cut off by the portcullis as it had fallen behind me. I had been riding the fore-part of the steed only. Of course that meant that the water was just pouring out of the beast as soon as he drank it!

I was very relieved when, at
this moment, the rest of my men
joined me. I was able to send several
of them to the Turks' fortress,
where they picked up the rear
portion of my mount and brought it
back to me.

One of the grooms in my force
had some skill with a needle, and he
was able to sew the two parts of Ajax
back together. For this purpose,
instead of thread he used young
shoots of a laurel bush. Later on,
after the wound had healed, these
shoots took root inside Ajax's body.
After a time these grew up over his
back in the form of a leafy arch, so
that even in the hottest weather I
was able to ride in the shade.

It was not only on land that I encountered strange creatures.
Once, while travelling by sea, I had the misfortune to be swallowed by
a whale.

It was a fine day off the coast of France, and while our ship was at
anchor I took the chance to dive over the side for a pleasant swim. No
sooner had I entered the water than I saw this great whale bearing
down on me, his jaws opened wide. In a second he had swallowed
me.

It was dark and warm in the stomach of the whale, but I decided
that I did not really want to stay there. I set about causing the creature
as much pain as possible, so that he would be glad to throw me back
up into the sea. Accordingly I danced and jumped as heavily as I
could. None of my movements, however, seemed to disturb him, for
the great whale kept on cruising calmly on, while I tired myself out in
his great stomach.

Then I had one of those strokes of fortune which have followed
me all through my life. An Italian ship, hunting whales, came across
my captor. They followed him and speared him to death with their
harpoons. This they followed by hauling the great creature up on to
the deck of their ship, while I remained a prisoner in the stomach of
the dead beast.

I could hear the crew of the ship preparing to cut up the body of the whale. This threw me into a panic. It was quite possible that their great knives and saws would cut me up at the same time!

In an effort to preserve my life I stood as near the centre of the stomach as possible. To my great relief the seamen started by slitting the whale's stomach from the bottom. As soon as the first glimmer of light appeared I shouted out loudly. You can imagine the amazement of the sailors when out of the stomach of the whale appeared a full-grown man, who bowed to them civilly and thanked them for delivering him from almost certain death.

Those good sailors fed me and allowed me to rest, and then took me back to the vessel on which I had been sailing. As far as I can tell, I was in the whale's stomach for almost five hours.

From the sunny seas off the shores of France the vessel took me, in good time, to the frozen seas of the great northern waters. While sailing past many icebergs one day, I saw through my telescope a large white polar bear. We were very short of meat so I had myself set aground on the iceberg. I then approached the great bear and shot it.

Unfortunately the report of my musket alerted thousands of bears who had been asleep on the ice. I could see them approaching in the distance, and knew that unless I thought of something quickly my last moment would soon be at hand.

Swiftly I took my hunting knife from my belt. With a few swift strokes I skinned the bear I had shot, kicking the carcase of the dead bear through a hole in the ice. I then wrapped the skin of the bear around me, putting my head under the bear's.

Soon all the other bears came nosing up to me, sniffing at my fur and touching me gently with their paws. Evidently they took me for the one I had shot, because they seemed to accept me as one of themselves. For my part I imitated their actions as best I could, until the time came that night for me to slip away from the others and get back to the small boat, in which I rowed thankfully back to the vessel.

As it happened, I got home from that voyage not by sea, as I had left, but by air. It happened in this way. I had gone ashore again one day and had climbed a tall hill. At the top of this hill was a large hole. I stood astride the hole and idly dropped a stone into it. I was not aware of this, but there was an eagle at the bottom of the hole. My stone disturbed her so greatly that she flew out of the hole in a great flurry. As I was standing astride the hole as she came out, the eagle bore me away with her on her back.

We flew for many days in this fashion, pausing to rest at night. Unfortunately for me, each time that the eagle stopped to rest it was on the top of a high mountain, so that I could not escape, but had to get on her back the next day in order to continue my journey.

I lost all count of time, but set my mind to overcoming my problem. After a great deal of thought I discovered that by pulling at the eagle's head I could change the direction in which she was flying. I plotted a course by the stars, and in this way got her to take me quite close to my home and to land me on a flat piece of land, before she flew off again.